Walt Disney Productions'

# Mickey's Christmas Carol

## GOLDEN PRESS • NEW YORK
### Western Publishing Company, Inc., Racine, Wisconsin

Poor Bob Cratchit! Mr. Scrooge had made him work late
again—even though it was Christmas Eve. But now, at last, he
could go home. "Merry Christmas!" he called.

"Christmas, bah!" shouted Scrooge.
"Don't forget to take my laundry."

Bob lugged the heavy laundry bag through the icy streets. He stopped once to rest, but only for a moment. When he thought of his family waiting for him, he picked up the bundle and trudged on.

"It's Papa!" cried Tiny Tim joyfully as Bob struggled through the door.

"Dinner will be ready soon, dear," said Mrs. Cratchit as she put some scraps into a pan. "I wish Mr. Scrooge would pay you more....He certainly has enough money."

But Scrooge *never* thought he had enough money. Tonight, as always, he had stayed late at the office to count his gold coins.

His nephew, Fred, opened the door.
"Here's a holly wreath for you, Uncle," he said. "I've come to invite you to Christmas dinner. We're having roast goose and plum pudding and candied fruits and..."

"Out of my way, boy," shouted Scrooge. "You know I can't eat that stuff!"

"Give a penny for the poor?" asked a man out on the street.
"Give *that* to the poor!" cried Scrooge angrily, shoving the wreath over the man's head.

"All this Christmas fuss," muttered Scrooge. "Bah, humbug."
He thought of his old, dead partner, Jacob Marley. "Marley never
gave anything away," he said. "He was my kind of man."

Scrooge shivered. He couldn't wait to get inside his warm
house.

As soon as he was indoors, Scrooge sank into
his favorite chair. He was just dozing off when—

*CLANK, CLANK, CLANK.*

Scrooge sat up with a start. The ghost of Jacob Marley was coming toward him, slowly dragging long, heavy chains.

"I must carry these chains through eternity," moaned Marley, "because I was selfish. Your punishment will be the same, Ebenezer Scrooge."

"No!" said Scrooge. "It can't be. Help me, Jacob."

"Tonight," said Marley, "three spirits will visit you. Listen to them, or your chains will be heavier than mine."

The ghost vanished. Scrooge blinked and shook his head. "I need rest," he thought. "Imagine—thinking I saw old Marley!" He climbed into bed.

He had barely fallen asleep when the alarm clock jangled. Scrooge opened his eyes and saw a dapper little fellow standing on the night table.

"I am the Ghost of Christmas Past," he said.

The ghost held out his hand. "Hold on," he said. "I'll take you to a Christmas of long ago."

Scrooge felt himself drift toward the ceiling. "Oh, oh, OHH!" he shouted as they sailed out the window.

They flew across the night sky and landed near a house filled with music and cheerful voices. Scrooge looked in the window. "Why, that's *me*," he gasped, "when I was young. And there's old Fezziwig. He gave me my first job. And there's my lovely Isabel."

"See how happy you were then, Scrooge," said the ghost. "You were full of love. But then you grew greedy and lost all your friends—even Isabel."

Scrooge turned away. "I don't want to see any more. Please, Spirit, take me home."

*Ring! Ring!* It was the alarm clock again. Scrooge opened his eyes. "I must have been dreaming," he said.

"Fee, fi, fo, fum!" boomed a voice. Across the room, a giant was sitting in Scrooge's chair, surrounded by bowls and platters of luscious-looking food.

"What's all this?" demanded Scrooge.

"It's the food of generosity," said the giant, "something you know nothing about. I'm the Ghost of Christmas Present. Come and see what's happening tonight." He picked Scrooge up and dropped him into his deep pocket.

Outside, the giant set Scrooge down in front of a tiny tumbledown house. Scrooge peered through a cracked window. "It's the Cratchits!" he said. "What a measly dinner they're having. Why aren't they eating the food in the bubbling pot?"

"That's your laundry," said the giant. "They're boiling it to make sure it gets extra clean."

"What's wrong with the lad?" asked Scrooge.

"Tiny Tim is very ill," said the giant. "He needs good food to make him strong and well. Pay his father more so he can buy his family enough to eat...." The giant's voice faded, and then he was gone.

Scrooge tried to call the giant back, but it was too late. Suddenly he was surrounded by thick clouds of smoke. When the air cleared, he was standing near a broken-down tombstone in a shadowy graveyard.

"Hello, Scrooge," said a voice behind him. "I am the Ghost of Christmas Future."

Scrooge turned to the ghost. "Whose lonely grave is this?" he asked.

"See for yourself," said the ghost. "It belongs to a man who was very rich. But he was so selfish and unkind that he had no friends."

Scrooge bent to read the name on the stone. "Ebenezer…
Scrooge. Oh, no! This is *my* grave!"

"That's right!" laughed the ghost.

"No, please," begged Scrooge. "I don't want to die all alone,
with no friends. I'll change my ways, I promise!"

"I'll change...." Scrooge's eyes flew open. He was in his own bed. He was still alive—and there was still time to change, to make a new beginning.

"It's Christmas morning!" he cried. He dressed quickly and rushed outside.

"Take these!" he called, tossing bags of money to the men collecting for the poor.

"Hello, Fred!" he shouted when he saw his nephew. "May I still come to dinner?"

"Of course, Uncle," replied Fred.

"Splendid! I'll see you later. There's something I must do first."

A while later, Scrooge knocked at Bob Cratchit's door.

"Merry Christmas!" Scrooge said happily. "I have another bundle for you."

"M-more laundry, sir?" gulped Bob.

Scrooge laughed. "Don't be silly, my boy!"

"Look, Papa," cried Tiny Tim, opening the sack. "Toys!"

"Friends are worth more than all the gold in the world," said Scrooge. "Cratchit, from now on you and your family will have all the good food and warm clothing you need. Merry Christmas, my friends!"

"And God bless us everyone!" shouted Tiny Tim.